The Boy with an R in His Hand

THE BOY WITH AN

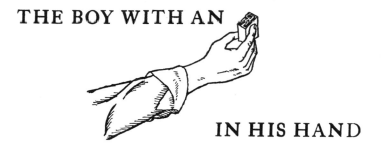

IN HIS HAND

*A tale of the type-riot
at William Lyon Mackenzie's
printing office in 1826*

BY JAMES REANEY

Illustrated by Leo Rampen

1965

MACMILLAN OF CANADA

TORONTO

Printed in Canada for The Macmillan Company of Canada Limited, 70 Bond Street, Toronto, by The Hunter Rose Co. Limited.

To James Stewart and John Andrew

ACKNOWLEDGMENT

The author wishes to thank Miss Edith Firth of the Toronto Public Library and Professor Frederick Armstrong of the History Department, Middlesex College, University of Western Ontario, for their very generous help in explaining to him how it was *then*.

CONTENTS

The Boy with an R in His Hand

【 1 】

THE BOYS ARRIVE
AT MUDDY LITTLE YORK

MORE than a hundred years ago, on a warm summer afternoon, the steamship *Canada* paddle-wheeled into the harbour of York. Two boys, one taller, one shorter, leaned against the rail and watched the lighthouse-keeper come out on his little balcony. With a long pole he raised a bright red flag high into the air, higher than the top of the lighthouse itself.

'Jo, why's he doing that?' asked Alec, who was the shorter boy. His older brother didn't know. Farther down the rail was a man in a yellow waistcoat and Alec asked him.

'He's signalling to the harbour-master that we're coming,' replied the man in the yellow waistcoat. 'We're coming in from Niagara, so we rates a red flag. If we was coming in from Kingston you'd see a blue flag, and if we was just a schooner he'd put up a white flag.'

'Are you from the States?' asked Alec after a second's pause.

'I was born here, young fellow, but Ma and Pa and me cleared out before the war. I'm out of Oswego right now. In the State of New York.'

'Never ask personal questions, Alec,' whispered Joel, who was blushing.

'I'm sorry. But – there's just one more thing. Have you got clocks in that box you have with you?'

'Is one of them ticking?' the Yankee said, cocking an ear. 'Why, yes, I'm a clock-pedlar and I've been selling clocks to you Canadians all summer long. You wouldn't care to buy a clock would you, little feller?'

Alec looked at Joel, but Joel shook his head and gave a tug at the back of Alec's shirt so as to twitch him away.

'Thank you for telling me about the flag,' said Alec, turning to look at the town, which could be clearly seen for the first time.

There seemed to be countless houses and buildings at York. Alec's breath was quite taken away. He could see some boys running down to the wharf – to watch the steamboat come in, no doubt. Harbour gulls flew up to scream at the lake gulls that had accompanied them from Niagara. As the ship splashed by a low sandy beach near the lighthouse, Alec's sharp eyes saw a heron fishing, an Indian boy running along a beach, and a woman shaking a duster out of a window – even a flock of wild ducks at the mouth of a little creek near the fort. But most of all he saw the houses.

'Isn't it grand, Joel! Look at the church with the tin rooster on top of it.'

The Yankee pedlar showed them where the court-

4

house was and where the rich people mostly lived, over near the Lieutenant-Governor's house and the fort. Tall green poplar trees grew in the yards of these houses and seemed to Alec to be tall green persons.

'Do you see that house with the wall around it?' asked the man in the yellow waistcoat. 'That's Doctor Strachan's house and it is filled with books and silver.'

There was a puff of smoke from the fort and a cannon boomed. The wild ducks flew up and away.

Also travelling on the *Canada* that late summer afternoon was a new coach that belonged to the Lieutenant-Governor and was being shipped across to him from Niagara where it had just been built. Sitting in the coach, so as to avoid contact with the vulgar mob, was a fine young English lady named Lady Catherine Figgis. She overheard Alec say that the town of York was grand.

'Hear that benighted infant,' she said to her maid, Betty, who stood at the coach door.

'I do, mum,' said Betty, who now turned up her nose at Alec.

'He calls this place grand!' went on the lady. 'Muddy Little York! The worst den I have ever seen in the whole civilized world. And yet' (here she yawned) 'I must last out another winter here and perhaps another, until Uncle Peregrine's term as governor of this wretched colony expires.'

'They're firing the cannon for your arrival, mum.'

'Oh, what a waste of powder. Tully, isn't it a waste of powder?' Tully was Lady Catherine's pet monkey. He was sitting in a corner of the coach and looked rather thoughtful.

'The reason we think it's so grand,' said Alec, sticking his head in the window, 'is that in the Red River Colony where we come from – miles and miles west of here, we've been three months coming from there in a canoe – why, there you scarcely see two houses stuck together and the prairie meadows are so big and flat, even one house doesn't seem lived in.'

'Oh!' shrieked Lady Catherine, flopping back on her cushions. 'Take the vulgar cub away. He smells like a weasel.'

'I'm sorry if I do,' said Alec, clinging hard to the edge of the window, for Joel was trying to pry him loose. 'Joel and I haven't seen a piece of soap now for three months and neither of us can swim.'

Just then the whistle of the *Canada* sounded and there was a sharp jerk as the paddle-wheels reversed. Lady Catherine shrieked a second shriek, but no one heard as there was noise and confusion enough, what

6

with the captain directing the lowering of two row-boats whose oarsmen were to pull the clumsy steamship up to the dock.

'Why can't I talk to the fine lady?' asked Alec as Joel dragged him away. 'Where I come from everybody is brothers and sisters. I want to ask her what the name of the animal she's got in there is.'

Joel's face turned crimson. He sometimes believed, and this proved it, that his younger brother had been sent into the world to embarrass him out of his wits at least once every day. Nay, twice a day.

Passengers were laughing at Alec's last remark, and

one old gentleman wearing a powdered wig said that there was no brother and sister nonsense in York, just master and servant.

Now further laughter and confusion broke out. Somehow or other, Alec had fallen over the rail.

But a young fellow fishing in a rickety boat was close enough to pull him out of the water almost right away. The moment the gangplank was down, Joel pushed his way past all the people ahead of him and, paying no attention to their complaints, ran along the wharf to where the fisherman was bringing in his brother.

〖 2 〗

BY THE WAY TO UNCLE JOHN'S

Y name's French, Charley French,' said the youth who had rescued Alec. He was taller than either of them, with a wide mouth fond of grinning, washed-out blue eyes, and sandy hair. Joel introduced himself and then opened their bundle to get out dry clothes for his brother. He apologized for his brother's carelessness.

'Say, fellow, why *did* you fall over? Were you trying to commit suicide? Were you heart-broken?'

Alec shook his head and smiled. He was watching the swallows dart back and forth from their nests in the sandy bank under the wharf. The swallows paid no attention either to them or to the crowd of people jostling on the wharf just above Alec's head. Some barrels were being rolled off the *Canada*. 'Wraump-wraump-wraump-wraumpity-wraump,' they said, as the men rolled them up the wharf.

'It was seeing that black man on the wharf,' laughed Joel. He wrung out Alec's wet clothes.

'That's Speakable Smith. He always comes down to see the boats come in. You folks never seen a black man before?'

Joel said no, they never had. He and his brother were from a part of the world where there had never been African slaves.

'Regular Garden of Eden, eh?' grunted French. He took a clay pipe out of his pocket and lit it skilfully from a tinder box that he took out of another pocket.

'Not always,' said Alec. He smoothed out the wrinkles in his buckskin leggings, which he hadn't been wearing since their coming to Niagara a week ago.

Just at this moment a particularly loud, rumbling sound overhead proclaimed the fact that Lady Catherine's coach was being rolled onto the wharf. Horses to pull it could be heard approaching. Through a crack between the boards they could see the gold glittering on the sides of the coach.

'Where you're from isn't even in Canada,' said French. He picked up the fish he'd caught.

'No. It isn't,' said Joel, feeling rather foreign.

What French said was true. The Red River Settlement was a separate British colony hundreds of miles away from the colonies known as the Canadas, Upper and Lower. The boys had just landed in the capital of Upper Canada.

'Well, you're in Canada now, boys, and I'll show you some of our choicest sights.' They walked out from under the wharf, scrambled up the bank and so onto the road that led into the town.

'But where were you going to?' asked French.

'We want to go to our uncle's place,' said Joel. 'His name's John Macalister.'

'John Simcoe Macalister, Esquire? That's a good kind of uncle to have.'

'Why?'

'They say he's going to be Chief Justice soon. Come on, I'll show you to his door. Are you fellows orphans or something like that?'

'Yes,' said Joel. 'Mother died when we were in Scotland. I don't know if Alec can remember her.'

'Oh, I can,' said Alec quietly. His eyes were kept very busy with all the new, strange things to see.

'We came out with father,' continued Joel, 'to the Red River Settlement. Do you know how we came out? It was in a sailboat and it was to another place called York, only it was York on Hudson Bay, not York on Lake Ontario.'

'I guess that's about a thousand miles away, isn't it?' said French.

'More than that. And then we came down quite a way, I guess, to Red River. Father stayed a while and then he left us with a Mr. Sutherland while he went off to preach to the Indians.'

'Was your father a *preacher*?' said French.

'Yes. Are you surprised?'

'Here, let me carry your bundle for you. It isn't every day I get to help fellows like you. What happened to your father?'

'The hunters came back in the fall with the story that the Sioux Indians had killed a white priest and some Salteaux Indians he was travelling with across the prairie. But our father had told Mr. Sutherland that if he did not come back, we should be sent to look up his brother-in-law John, down in Upper Canada. In the spring we came here with the voyageurs.'

'I can remember Scotland too,' announced Alec

suddenly. 'And I can remember that other place called
York. I can remember the people. They paddled about
in little boats called kayaks and they could turn side-
ways somersaults in them.'

'You're in Canada now,' said French, 'and I don't
advise you to try any more of them somersaults in the
water.'

Ahead of them moved the coach. It was preceded
and followed by other passengers who were going to
their various inns and houses, or perhaps to the stage-
coach office, or perhaps to the farms in the wilderness
north of the town. Joel felt that people were laughing
at them, particularly at Alec's buckskin leggings. Red
River clothes were much different from those worn in
Upper Canada and he dreaded being outlandish in any
way whatsoever.

Alec loved wearing his leggings and was relieved not
to have scratchy woollen pantaloons on any more.

Lady Catherine's coach turned off to the left towards the fort and towards Government House. On
the side of her conveyance, a coat of arms showed a
fierce lion and a unicorn with a sharp horn. Alec
thought they glared at him as the coach turned.

'Look at the earth, Joel,' said Alec kicking up the
dust of King Street. 'It's different from our earth back
home, isn't it?'

'What's your earth like?' asked French. He shifted
their bundle from one shoulder to another.

'Red River earth is black. Not brown like this. Hey,
Jo, look at all the people over there.'

To their left, there was a church with a spire and a
cross on top. Next were some red brick buildings that

French informed them were the new court-house and
the new jail. A crowd of people was gathered there –
horsemen, farmers in wagons – all with their backs to
the boys.

'They're watching a man getting hanged,' explained
French. 'It's – don't you see the gallows? They'll hang
him at four o'clock.'

'How awful to hang a man,' said Alec. 'No matter
what he's done. What has the poor, wretched creature
done to deserve this?'

'Killed somebody,' said Joel. 'You have to be hanged
if you've murdered someone.'

'Well,' said French mysteriously.

They turned down King Street and Alec remarked
on all the curious signs over the shop doors. One house
had a large wooden boot hanging over its door, and
the boot had a crown on it.

'That's the shoemaker's,' explained French. 'That's
a thing you'll soon find out about around here. You
may have wondered why some of those loafers were

joking about you down at the wharf, but you see it's your moccasins. Don't you ever wear shoes?'

The boys looked down at their feet and it was almost as if they had been told that they had no toes. Yes, shameful it was, but true. For years now they had always worn moccasins. Joel resolved to get hold of some shoes right away, the moment he could get permission from Uncle John. Alec was still really thinking about the hanging. But the other signs that hung along the street soon drove the ideas of both hanging and moccasins from the boys' minds.

Over a carpenter's shop, there was a large cut-out wooden axe. Over the gunsmith's door, a giant rifle. Over the tailor's, a golden fleece, and over the blacksmith's, an anvil and hammer. Over the grocer's, a gilded tea chest; and last of all, at the fur-trading post, a huge picture of a ferocious Indian with a tomahawk in his hand and some skins hanging down from his belt.

Suddenly there was a flurry of hooves, and French yelled at them to get out of the way. A horseman had nearly ridden them down from behind. They could hear him laughing through the clouds of dust that rose up behind his horse, and Alec's shoulder stung where the rider's whip had struck him.

'Who is he and why did he do that?' asked Alec.

'Jarvis,' replied French. 'He likes riding down any apprentice of Mr. Mackenzie. He had Jim Baxter limping around for about a week.'

'Are you an apprentice? Who's Mr. Mackenzie?' asked Joel all in one breath.

'Who's this Jarvis?' interrupted Alec.

13

'You'll find out,' said French.

'Why does he ride you down?'

'Mr. Jarvis is a Tory. My master, Mr. Mackenzie, is a Reformer. He prints a paper that says them Tories run the government for themselves and not for the people. So all their young blades try to chase Mackenzie's boys off the road.'

'What on earth is a Tory?' asked Alec.

'Perhaps you should leave Mr. Mackenzie's office,' said Joel gravely. 'You might get killed by these Tory riders.'

'I can't leave,' said French, 'because I'm sworn to work in his printing office until I'm twenty years old. So I'll take my chance. You want to know what a Tory is?'

By this time the apprentice of Mackenzie and rescuer of Alec had guided them up a side street where he paused at a spot across the road from a handsome brick house. They soon understood this to be their uncle's house.

'Here's a Tory's house,' said French, handing over the bundle to Joel. 'You ask him what a Tory is. Better not tell him an apprentice of Mackenzie's helped you to his door, or he may throw you out. There's one thing, though. You know that Jarvis that rode us down? When he was a young fellow he killed another lad, younger than he was, in a duel. But did he hang for it? No. For one reason and another – mainly because his father was Provincial Secretary.'

'But he killed somebody. Surely – ' Joel was puzzled.

'Wait a second. You know the guy they're hanging today? Old Isaac Worden. Did he kill somebody? No. Do you know what he killed?'

'No,' said Joel. Joel didn't know whether he liked his uncle being called a Tory or not. 'How could we know? We only just came here.'

'You know why they're hanging him? Because he stole and slaughtered a cow.'

The boys were too astonished to say anything to

15

this, and before they could say good-bye to French he had walked down the street beneath the shadow of some huge willow trees, come out into the sunlight again, and turned sharply right on King Street where he disappeared from view.

[3]

THE GIRL WITH AN R
ON HER HAND

UNCLE John's house was of red brick and set in a large garden, which at the back became almost a small farm. There was a pigeon house, a sheep house, a poultry house, and, off to one side, a swine house or pig-sty. There was also a stable for the horses that pulled Uncle John's coach. The coachman who drove these horses lived up above them.

The garden was laid out in square beds joined together with gravelled paths. Alec had never seen so many kinds of flowers and vegetables; and for the first time he saw apple and pear trees, trees not seen in the Red River country with its colder winters.

The windows of Uncle John's house were larger than any the boys had seen out west. As if they might be a sort of game, they were made up of many small square panes of glass, and Alec thought of the rain playing checkers upon them. Up over the front door was a pretty flower-like window, which Cousin Bathsheba called a fanlight. Up above this, set in the gable of the house, was a small oval window they called a bull's-eye window.

Inside, Uncle John's house was just as splendid as
outside – with marble fireplaces, crystal chandeliers,
and walls painted with festoons of flowers and ruined
Grecian temples. In one room there was a dark green
carpet. This was called the drawing-room, although
Alec never observed that anyone did any drawing
there. In the room called the parlour, there was a
bright red carpet on the floor. Alec felt his head swim-
ming at all the colour and sparkle.

Directly underneath the parlour was the kitchen, a
basement kitchen, and two maidservants carried trays
of food up and down a steep, narrow pair of stone
stairs. Here Alec and Cousin Allan ate their supper.
Alec kept looking at the fire in the great fireplace. He
thought of all the campfires he and Joel had fallen
asleep by as they came down the rivers and lakes with

the voyagcurs. If he closed his eyes he could still hear the singing and hear the paddles dripping in the cold flowing water.

Joel had been thought old enough to have tea with Aunt Henrietta and Uncle John upstairs. Alec was just as glad he had been kept down in the kitchen, for he was mortally afraid of breaking one of Aunt Henrietta's china cups. Down in the kitchen they ate off tin plates and he was safe, or so he thought, from any further embarrassing accidents such as had made his first minutes at York so memorable and so watery.

'Let's ask to go out after supper,' said Cousin Allan. 'Let's go and tease the bear in Gosling's yard.'

Alec looked at his cousin, who wasn't too much older than he was. Cousin Allan had curly blond hair, a little snub nose, and a mouth that never quite closed over two large, white, upper front teeth.

'How come he keeps a bear in his yard?'

'He caught it when it was a cub and he put it in a cage. He lets us tease it with sticks and stones.'

'Sounds cruel. I'd not like it,' replied Alec. 'Joel and I don't believe in torturing animals. My father says that some day there must be no traps and no gallows, and babies will play with lions and lions with babies.'

'Aw, come off that preaching stuff. Hey, I'm going to call you Reverend. Say, a fat lot of good all that talk did your father. He got scalped by Indians, didn't he? Isn't that right, Rev?'

'No one knows exactly what happened to Father,' said Alec. 'Except that he disappeared and the hunters came back with their story.'

Cousin Allan then suggested that they take his fighting rooster, Napoleon, over to Fisty Jarvis's stable and watch it fight a certain renowned black rooster that lived there. But Alec thought this was just as cruel as the proposal to go torment a bear.

'Well then, Reverend,' exploded Cousin Allan, 'what in blazes' name do you want to do after supper?'

'I'd like to explore the town.'

'Oh, Reverend, what a muff you are! Explore the town. Who wants to do that? Here I thought I'd have someone to play with.'

'So did I,' said Alec, whose quick tongue was soon to get him into trouble.

'You needn't give yourself airs, Reverend. You're only an orphan now, you know. And if Papa doesn't educate you, you may have to grow up to be a labourer. I'll be a gentleman when I grow up, but you'll have to work with your hands.'

'Who cares,' said Alec. 'It's a free country. Say, Allan, what's the name of the girl over there who's slicing the bread?'

'Rebecca.'

'What's the matter with her hand?' whispered Alec. 'She's got such a funny mark on the back of her hand.'

Cousin Allan grinned and then shouted at the servant-girl to come over and show young Reverend her hand. Alec, for embarrassment, could have fallen through the floor.

'See her hand?' cried Allan grabbing it. 'It's got an R branded on it – do you know why?'

'Please,' said Alec hiding his face. 'Don't tell me. Please forgive me, Rebecca.'

'It's because she's a robber. Aren't you, Rebecca? So, R for Robber.'

It came out that last year the girl had been working at Doctor Strachan's, whose great house Alec had seen as they sailed into the harbour. One day Mistress Strachan noticed that one of her best silver spoons was missing, and Rebecca was accused of stealing it. Rebecca said that she had known the spoon to be missing for some time, but had been afraid to tell how it had disappeared because it was such a strange story.

Her story was that all one morning she had noticed a crow hanging about the windows, sitting on window sills and occasionally croaking at her. The windows were open, since it was the first fine weather they had had, and Mistress Strachan had wanted the house to be aired. She directed Rebecca to clean the silver and then went off in the carriage to tea at another lady's

house. The spoons were cleaned last and lay ready on a table. Rebecca left the room for a few minutes to answer the door. When she came back one of the spoons was missing.

'A likely story,' said Allan.

'But true, Master Allan,' said Rebecca firmly.

'Shut up. Well, Reverend, the Strachans and the court didn't believe that story, especially when a silver pin of Mrs. Strachan's had also disappeared. Where'd you bury them, Rebecca? So she was convicted of stealing these things herself – let that be a lesson to you, Reverend! We don't like robbers in York. So they took a branding-iron with R on it for ROBBER and heated it up in the stove at the court-house, and then took this very hand and stamped R on it forever.'

'Rebecca,' came Bathsheba's voice from the top of the stairs. 'You had best bring up the tea now, and Papa wants to see you, Cousin Alec.'

As they climbed up the steps and proceeded to the drawing-room, Alec had a chance to apologize to the girl.

'It doesn't matter, Master Alec. You couldn't help it.'

'Rebecca, I believe you about the crow. Out on the Red River there was a raven stole a ring once from the Governor's lady. She left it out on a table with the window open. Maybe I'll find the spoon and the pin for you some day. They caught the raven, you know, and she got her ring back. Everyone had been saying it was the Indians.'

'That's very kind of you, Master Alec,' whispered Rebecca, as they came to the end of the passageway and so to the door of the drawing-room. Rebecca set down the Macalisters' great silver teapot, which was decorated with a large capital M and even a coat of arms.

At first when they had seen their Uncle John's face they had thought how much he looked like their mother! He was their mother's brother after all. But there were two heavy lines that came down from either side of his nose to the corners of his mouth. Their mother's face had been kind. But his voice was growly, and his mouth was always twisting into a scornful smile at those he spoke to, as if he didn't think they were his equals.

'Well, boy,' said Uncle John to Alec. 'What did your father think I should do to help his orphans?'

'I don't know,' said Alec, looking at the teapot. 'Send us to school maybe.'

'Call me *sir*, if you please.'

'Address your Uncle John as *sir*,' put in Aunt Henrietta. Aunt Henrietta had very blond, almost white-blond, hair nearly hidden by a large beruffled and belaced white cap. The ladies who lived on the banks of the Red River had worn such caps, but never as full and as foaming with lace as Aunt Henrietta's.

'Call him *sir*,' whispered Joel.

'School, boy?' went on Uncle John. 'Where would I get the money?'

'Father sent money along with us. Didn't you give him the sealed letter, Joel? Oh – pardon me, Uncle John – Sir John, I mean.'

'Not enough. Enough for a couple of years. But not for more than that.'

'Feeding two growing boys is no easy thing with prices the way they are in this town. Tch-tch-tch-tch,' put in Aunt Henrietta with a headshake.

'Quiet, Etta. Quiet till I tell the cub what I could do with him and his brother here. After all, how do I know you really are my nephews?'

'Well, who are we then?' said Alec, forgetting to say 'sir' already. 'Where did we get the letter and the box with Father's papers in them? And Mother's things.'

'Why, you might be two vagabond boys who stole their things.' There was a twinkle in Uncle John's eyes. It was his idea of joking with his nephews. 'Now, boys, I own a grist-mill and a large piece of farm property up the river, and my people up there are always asking if I could send them up some young

lads to help. If you don't turn out well down here –
you at my office, Joel, and you at the school, Alec – I'll
send you up there and let the miller take care of you.
How do you like the sound of that?'

'Not much,' said Alec.

Both Aunt and Uncle haw-hawed at this. Alec could
see their reflections bobbing up and down in the silver
sides of the teapot, as Aunt Henrietta poured out tea
for everyone.

'Sounds too much like hard work, eh?' roared Uncle
John, slapping his knee and laughing some more. 'By

the way,' he continued, suddenly changing, 'there's one thing – nephews, let me remind you. You come from an outlandish part of the world where, no doubt, you had tea with Indians and ate off the same plate as the buffaloes. But now you're in civilized society. So – well? Alec, I saw you talk familiarily with our servant-girl, Rebecca. Never talk with servants or criminals. Give them orders, yes; talk with them, no. Always remember what a well-bred family the Macalisters are. Empire Loyalist. A family to be proud of.'

'Why,' laughed Alec. 'Why, Uncle John, our father always told us that your father – Mother's father – was a farrier, a man who takes care of horses when they're sick, a farrier in the army till our other grandfather gave him the money to start his store here.'

'Your maternal grandfather,' roared Uncle John, 'was a distinguished surgeon, you young lout!'

'I'm sure he was. He drew out Governor Simcoe's bad teeth for him, but he started out on horses.'

At this point Uncle John gave Alec a series of smart cuffs and fell into a terrible fit of temper. Uncle John did not like to be reminded that his father had been a farrier. 'Off to your garret – show him up, Bathsheba, before he's the first nephew I've ever thrashed,' he said, when his roars had become speech again.

Alec fled the room and seemed asleep in bed when Joel came up later on in the evening. But Alec said good-night from under the covers.

'I'm not going to say good-night to you,' said Joel. 'You embarrassed me twice today and you're such a little fool. We've got to get along with these people. We've got to.'

Joel got into bed, blew out the candle, and burrowed his head into the bolster.

Joel was in many ways quite different from Alec. Alec thought over the differences. It had not been a pleasant evening. After recovering from Uncle John's cuffs, Alec had heard the bear, growling in its cage somewhere not far off, and the shouts of the boys as they roused its fury with sticks and stones.

Yes, Joel and he were different. For example, when the cannon had been fired that afternoon at the fort Joel's heart had beat with fear, but Alec's with joy at the marvellous sound.

Joel slept soundly tonight, because for the first time since they had come to North America he was sure that Indians, wild Indians, would not attack, could not attack. But Alec almost prayed nightly that the Indians would attack and kidnap him. He was ready to admit that they might kill him, but then there were those lucky white infants who were adopted into savage tribes. He would be one of those and be a happy Indian for the rest of his life. For him the trip down through the wilderness had been disappointingly peaceful.

As for having to stay and live with these people, thought Alec, also thinking how he must get up early in the morning and do something about that bear, as for having to live with these people, surely that wasn't true. Surely you could always run away.

[4]

A BEAR FROM ITS CAGE

VERY early the next morning, while the houses and yards of Uncle John's street were swathed in a cool, light fog, someone must have been tinkering with the door to the bear cage in Gosling's yard, because a few moments later, looming rather larger than life because of the fog, the bear itself appeared in the Macalister yard and helped himself to some of the beehives that were standing in a corner by some currant bushes. After scraping the honey out of three hives and paying no attention whatsoever to the bees, who were thunderously angry at such an early awakening, the bear crashed through the fence, and could be seen crossing a field and then disappearing into the forest, leaving a trail of honey smears and disturbed bees.

'Hello, Alec,' said Cousin Bathsheba a half-hour later as she met Alec walking about the garden. 'Do you like to walk about in the early morning, too? There's been a bear at the beehives. Won't Father be angry!'

Luckily the mist was still thick enough to prevent a really good light falling on Alec's face, which had a rather curious expression on it at that very moment.

'Do you like walking in the garden?' asked Bath-sheba, starting the conversation again.

'Oh yes,' said Alec. 'I've never been in such a beautiful place in all my life.'

'You must come and look at my little garden.' Bathsheba's plot was thickly growing with plants, but at first they did not seem interesting to Alec since they did not have flowers.

'Have your flowers come up, Bathsheba?' he said frowning.

'Oh yes,' she laughed. 'It's an herb garden. All the plants have different leaves if you look at them closely, and they smell and taste differently too.' She plucked

and crushed a lavender leaf and gave it to him to smell.

Dimly, Alec could recall a certain good dress of his mother's smelling like this, although the lavender that so scented it had been grown in a far-away country.

Bathsheba looked at him quietly as he held the leaf to his nose. She had a nice wide mouth with a pleasant smile, and since she was impatient of wearing a bon-

net, her face was lightly dusted with freckles her
mother highly disapproved of.

'Alec,' she said at length. 'Would you promise me
something? I am going away to school in a fortnight.
Yes, all the way to Montreal, and I shan't be able to
harvest my garden. Could you take care of it for me
and send me the lavender after you've threshed out
the seeds? I want to make presents to some of my
friends at school. And one of my teachers said she

could not believe that York could grow any herbs. I want to show her up, but I'm having to leave before they're ripe.'

'Sure,' said Alec, kneeling down to look more closely at the odd little plants, some with sharp spiky leaves and others with thick, sad-looking, blotched and speckled leaves.

Cousin Bathsheba taught him all there was to know about her garden. The mist thinned off, the sun showed, and shadows began to come on, long early-morning shadows, rapidly shortening as the sun got higher. A flock of crows flew cawing over the sky and wheeled about the church spire at the crossroads of the town. From the spire the bell rang out seven times.

'Dearest Daughter,' wrote Aunt Henrietta that fall to Bathsheba far away in Montreal.

Dearest Daughter,

Father and I were most happy to hear from you, and I hasten to write this to catch the last boat out of here to Montreal before the ice and winter freeze us in. Your little cousin is most anxious that I send you off your parcel of weeds, and I hope that Miss Edgar does not mind your strange liking for seeds and plants.

Your big cousin, since you ask after their welfare, is doing very well in Father's office and has been most useful and obedient. But little Alec has been rather a mystery and bewilderment to us. What would you say of a boy who refused to be whipped by Mr. Aiken, the headmaster at the school? I will admit that he did not deserve the whipping but happened to be the first boy the master could lay his hands on – the other lads had locked Mr. Aiken out of the school and run off when he finally broke through their barricade. All but

Master Alec who kicked his shins when the poor man attempted to whip him.

Since he would not go back to the school, Father said he must go and work for his living at the Mill, and we were about to send him to the Mill when two more incidents occurred which speeded him on his way. Master Allan, who is incorrigibly naughty, had stolen some eggs one day to throw at a wretched woman locked up in the pillory at the Market Place. Your Cousin Alec chose to buffet against Allan in such a way that all of the eggs broke in Allan's coat pocket and made his best school coat a nasty omelette.

But worse is to follow. After my calling on the Lieutenant-Governor's niece, Lady Catherine Figgis – you may remember, with you, late in the summer – you said you could not bear her artificial ways, but my dear girl, everyone cannot hoe gardens and moon about the river marsh collecting plants the natural way you affect – finally, I heard her coach stop by our little house and knew that Lady Catherine was at last going to return my call.

All was proceeding quite civilly until, somehow or other, a huge gentleman pig appeared in the Drawing Room and made as if to drink from a teacup. I had sent your Cousin Alec on an errand to buy me some tea which I was very short of, and he had forgot to shut the Court-yard gate. Of course, one of the pigs running loose in the town, one of those seen to wallow at the Market Place no doubt, one of *those* pigs got into our court through the open gate and so pushed its way into the house and so into my Drawing Room, the first pig ever there I think. Lady Catherine fainted away at the mere sight, her little dog Flora has been ill ever since, and her Monkey, called Tully I believe – the first Monkey I believe also to visit my Drawing Room – a

detestable creature – ran up the chimney and onto our roof from which it could barely be induced to come down. The serving-girls said they could barely sleep for the creature pattering back and forth on the roof all night till morning. Young Alec, I will admit, is very good with animals and beckoned the Pig out, and was the only one the Monkey would listen to, he climbing up out of the bull's-eye window to try and trap it down, which he did. But he did leave the Gate open. Lady Catherine says she met my nephew on the boat this summer and had certainly hoped never to renew the acquaintance, but she was forced to thank him for getting her Monkey down, an animal she esteems very much and had quite despaired of ever seeing close up again.

The next scampish thing you will certainly not believe. You may remember that wretched levelling Scotsman, Mackenzie, who runs the printing-shop and prints the paper Father despises, although he subscribes. Mr. Mackenzie advertised for an apprentice, and your Cousin Alec had the temerity to go down and apply without consulting either his Aunt or his Uncle. He said that he would rather learn how to print than to grind corn, but his Uncle John had him chastised and sent up to the Mill, our bailiff Mr. Jakes coming down for him in a cart. I could not make the boy understand that, of course, our family would never allow even an orphan to work for that wretched trouble-maker Mackenzie, who is always stirring up the common people against the Government.

To make it short, Cousin Alec has run away from the Mill, been caught and returned once. Now the people at the Mill say that they do not want him at the Mill any longer. There is nothing but disaster following his stay there. Something to do with letting pigs into the Mill I believe, one of them ground in with the flour for all I know – the boy's name should be Eumaeus, not Alexander, after the old swineherd who recognizes Odysseus, you know. So, to cap it all, your Father in a perfectly towering rage went to Mackenzie and told him if he wanted Alec as an apprentice he could have him.

My dear Bathsheba, you can imagine my dismay when it seemed that Father was absolutely bent on getting my nephew Alec right out of the house, for if he were apprenticed to Mr. Mackenzie he would very probably sleep and eat at Mackenzie's, and so be completely lost to us his relatives. And grow up under the complete influence of that nasty agitator. After my tears, your Father consented to letting Alec live with us still while he apprentices, and I gather that Mackenzie is good enough to see that his lads go to a school that meets in the evenings. Father rather expects that little Alec might some day be very useful to him and to the Government as our little spy in the enemy camp, but I don't think this will ever turn out.

One thing I will say for Alec, he is willing and will do things for me and help. Whereas you will remember how Allan would never bring in a chip of wood when we lived in the smaller house, even though the fire might be stony cold and black.

My dear girl, when Mrs. Brant invites you to tea remember me particularly to her. We were girls together in the town you are now in. When you reply to this, it will be winter and I suppose the stage will bring your letter all the long way to York through the snowy wilderness up the road from Quebec.

Yours affectionately,
Mother

P.S. I enclose a thread of the colour I want. It is called garter Blue, and when you see what I will do with it in your Christmas box you will be very happy that you sent your mother directly about three skeins or an ounce of same.

[5]

CROAKER

EARLY one October afternoon, the sky was grey as an old board with the sun in it like a dim yellow knot-hole. A short, red-haired man came inquiring after Alec at the Macalisters' house. It was a Sunday afternoon and the frost had come early.

'You're somewhat older than I thought,' said Mr. Mackenzie. 'Are you the orphan boy Mr. Macalister said I might have as my apprentice?'

'No, sir. I'm Joel Buchanan. It's my brother Alec you want. He's up at my uncle's mill on the river.'

'I must go and get him then, mustn't I?'

'Yes. Poor Alec. He doesn't seem to get along with any of his masters.'

'I liked his handwriting. And the way he wrote. I may be the master he will get along with. How long is it since you've seen your brother?'

'Two months.'

'Would you like to come along with me and we'll bring him back together? Come, lad, step up into the seat beside me.'

Joel took a hasty look around him, for he did not want Uncle John to see him in Mr. Mackenzie's company. But there seemed to be no one looking out any of the windows, nor did there seem to be anybody about the streets. Joel stepped up into Mr. Mackenzie's gig.

Soon Mr. Mackenzie's wheels were singing over the frosty road. From time to time as the horse's hooves came down on it, the thin ice over the puddles broke and tinkled. They passed the toll-gate, rattled over the bridge, and then turned north on a road that went through a dense forest, sometimes close to the river bank and at other times swerving away from it. Joel

felt uneasy under some of Mr. Mackenzie's clear, penetrating looks. He should have tried to see Alec long ago, but then his uncle had made such a pet of him and found Alec such a burden that it was hard to be a brother and a nephew all at the same time. And then too, Joel was afraid to walk in the forest all alone. He could never have made it to the mill up this dark road.

Joel did not look back into Mr. Mackenzie's eyes, but he did occasionally look at him, long enough to ascertain that Mr. Mackenzie's red hair was in reality a rather old red wig.

They ducked down to avoid a low-hanging branch of a great buttonwood tree, so huge that the road had been made to go around it.

That same afternoon Alec sat in the kitchen of the miller's house polishing at a silver buckle he had acquired in a swap with another boy when he had still been living in town. Any real use the buckle might be put to had never occurred to him until that morning, when the miller's wife happened to mention that her pet crow had once run away on them, or rather flown away, and only by sheerest chance had been caught again in the near-by woods. This had made Alec wonder if the crow had escaped the miller and his wife at a time when people would be spring-cleaning in the town, polishing silver spoons that would glint in the sunlight to a pair of greedy eyes at the top of a tree.

'Millie, dear,' croaked a voice from high up in the chimney corner. 'Shall I come in to breakfast now?'

Hopping back and forth in a willow cage, sometimes sticking his large beak and head out through the withes, was a tame crow that had been taught to talk, as tame crows sometimes can. What this crow said was mostly the overheard conversation of the miller and his wife, although Alec always wondered if the crow had not thought up some of his speeches by himself. For example: 'Grind the barley, Charley!' and 'Oh, bless my poor old bones!' Sometimes he would talk the way Mr. Jakes did. Mr. Jakes was Uncle John's man, who stayed at the mill and watched that the miller and his wife ran it properly, for they were in debt to Uncle John and had to run the mill for him in order to pay off their debt. When Mr. Jakes was in the crow's mind, the latter was apt to say things like 'Get a move on there! Get a move on!' or 'Look lively or I'll thump you one!' Alec had been teaching the crow to say 'Alec doesn't like it at Uncle John's mill,' but so far the bird had not responded.

Alec, after shining the buckle to a high state of polish, placed it on the table and then propped open the kitchen door. Next he opened the cage and stood by waiting to see what would happen.

He could hear the fire crackling on the hearth and hear the water gurgling through the mill-race. The crow, after a long inspection of the unfastened opening, hopped out of its cage and flew rather clumsily over to the table.

Alec had tied a long piece of red yarn to the buckle, and this seemed to bemuse the bird for some time. However, he overcame his suspicions of the yarn, picked up the buckle in his beak, and flapped out of the doorway and down the steps. Since the crow's wings had been clipped after his escape, Alec found it fairly easy to follow him, but he sometimes had to run and also to be very quick at spotting the yarn as the bird led him into the forest away from the mill.

Deeper in the forest, the pet crow, or Croaker as he was known to Alec, managed to shake off his follower, and Alec, humming to himself, seemed to forget his original purpose. Instead he now fell to picking up the butternuts and beechnuts that had lately fallen to the ground and were now almost covered over with fallen leaves.

After he had picked his pockets full of nuts, he lay down in the deep carpet of fallen leaves and read from a pocket Bible his mother had given him long ago for his birthday. In the tiny print his sharp eyes skimmed over the story of Jacob and Esau. He wondered if he and Joel would ever be like that. How mean it was of Jacob to get everything away from his brother.

After a while, Alec put away his Bible and knelt in the leaves with his arms on a boulder. He prayed as follows:

'Dear God, please let me leave here soon. I'm afraid of Mr. Jakes. I don't want to run away again. I don't like being alone at the mill when they're away and only Mr. Jakes is around.

'Please make Joel love me again and not be so mad at me.

'Please let me find Croaker. Is that him rustling about there? Please let him be the bird I suspect he is.

'And if I have to climb any trees please don't let me fall down.

'But chiefly – let me get away from Mr. Jakes and the mill here. Amen.'

After this, Alec got up and walked among the trees with a new sense of being about to find something. And although he found nothing, neither Croaker, nor buckle, nor red yarn, he still felt the excitement of something about to happen or be discovered.

A bluejay screamed. A squirrel chattered angrily at him from the top of an oak tree. A long straggly V of wild geese flew over, their harsh and cackling cries thrilling him to the bottom of his heart. How he longed to be back at the Red River where every fall the geese flew like this following the river south. The

sky began to grow darker. The shadowy tree trunks
around him appeared to grow larger. He leaned against
a dead tree and looked at the sunset through the dark
stems of the forest.

Far away, in a corner of the sky, there was a won-
derful chalky-pink light with tons of grey cloud pressing down on it from the north. Alec was just thinking
very reluctantly, as he looked at this, that he must
get back to the mill, when he saw the thread of red
yarn hanging from a branch of the dead tree. Croaker
was looking down at him from the splintered crown of
the tree, not too far from the ground, since the tree
had been broken in two by a storm a long time ago.

Alec began to inch his way up and soon looked Croaker
in the eye – and thought he did not look too pleased.
With a further squirm or two Alec was able to look
down into the dead tree.

The inside of the tree was hollow and contained a
large and frowzy nest made of twigs and reeds. At the
bottom of the nest, there stuck out something bright –
the silver buckle, which Croaker had just been hiding
there.

Alec searched with his hands through the weaving of the nest until he felt another smooth object – a silver pin, silver no longer, for the rains and snow of a year had tarnished the metal. Alec lifted out the nest and dropped it to the ground. Then he slid down pretty quickly, but not fast enough to beat Croaker, who flew down and pecked away at the nest himself.

'Alec!' came his brother's voice echoing through the still, leafless trees. Alec could see two figures coming up the path, one of them carrying a lantern. At last Uncle John had come for him, and Joel had come with him. Carrying the nest and holding on to Croaker he ran towards the light.

'Joel! Uncle John!'

'Oh, I'm not your Uncle John!' laughed Mr. Mackenzie. Yes, he was a much shorter man than Uncle John, and with a red wig on his head.

'Mr. Mackenzie and I drove up here to bring you back, Alec,' said his brother. 'Mr. Mackenzie wants you to be an apprentice in his printing-shop.'

'Oh I'm so glad,' said Alec. 'For I don't think they need me at the mill any longer. Mr. Jakes keeps saying he's going to tie me to the mill-wheel and I think he means it.'

'Well, I'll not let him do that,' said Mr. Mackenzie. 'What have you got there, lad?'

'It's a crow's nest,' said Alec. 'This is Mrs. Chaple's pet crow, Croaker. Look what I found in the nest.' Alec held up the silver brooch and Croaker introduced himself by asking Charley to grind the barley.

'What is the story behind this pin, lad?' asked Mr. Mackenzie.

'Why, you see, I think it's Mrs. Strachan's pin as was stolen from her a year or two ago. And I think that if you were to go through the nest you'd find her silver spoon.'

Mr. Mackenzie held up the lantern to see better. Their shadows, huge and tall, wavered against the tree trunks along the path.

On the way back to the mill the boys told Mr. Mackenzie about Rebecca and her story of how the spoon was really stolen. At the mill, Alec said good-bye to the miller and his wife, who had been loudly wondering where he and Croaker had got to. They had returned from a visit to find Croaker and boy gone, as well as fire out and kitchen door wide open.

Alec scarcely had time to calm them down.

Finally, just as Alec was climbing into the gig beside Mr. Mackenzie and Joel, he heard a horse galloping up the road from the town.

'Where ya takin' that boy?' said Mr. Jakes, dismounting from his horse. He was a hulking brute of a man, with shaggy black hair that still didn't quite cover the fact that Mr. Jakes had, at some time or other, lost both his ears. 'That boy's to stay here.'

'I'm not apprenticed to you,' said Alec.

'This boy's my boy,' said Mr. Mackenzie drily and shook the reins to get his horse going. 'Mr. Macalister told me to come up and get him. I see no reason why any child should be left to your care, Mr. Jakes, and I bid you good evening.'

Jakes roared out at this and padded along behind them for a few minutes, but at length gave up the chase. Alec wondered if Mr. Jakes would now pursue them on his horse, and when they came to the buttonwood tree he had a nervous dread that he saw the man lying up in the tree, waiting to tumble down on them as they passed under the low-hanging branch.

But nothing like this happened. Instead Mr. Mackenzie had them tell their story, how they had been orphaned in the Red River country and come down through the wilderness to Upper Canada. Mr. Mackenzie told how he too had lost his father early in life, in Scotland, and had been brought up by a loving mother who had sacrificed a great many things that her son might be educated. Alec asked him what Scotland was like, and Mr. Mackenzie told them of old, crowded cities, and blue distant hills, a land where there had not been a large forest for centuries and wolves were no more seen; where there was an old wall the Romans had built that marched over the hills from sea to sea, had built long before this new country had ever been dreamt of.

As they crossed over the bridge, the horse's hooves made a hollow sound that meant safety to Alec, but also the end of the talk. These two things were even more true after Mr. Mackenzie had paid the toll-gate keeper and the toll-gate was shut behind them. In the darkness now, the town of York was just a handful of sparks where people had lamps and candles lit at windows. As they came up to Uncle John's door, an owl cried a shivery cry.

'It's tomorrow morning I'll see you, mind,' said Mackenzie in parting to Alec, 'at eight o'clock sharp.'

Alec promised to be there. The two boys watched the lantern on Mr. Mackenzie's gig move away, grow smaller, and then disappear on the other side of the thick-branched willow trees.

When they turned towards the house the elegant windows seemed, to Alec, to frown at them.

'Where have you been?' said the study window on the left. 'And who have you been with?' asked the drawing-room window on the right.

46

[6]

HOW TO SET TYPE

ALEC was made an apprentice to Mr. Mackenzie the very next morning, and his first hours in the printing office on Palace Street made him sure that this was the life for him.

In the shop there were four boys of his own age, two more of about Joel's age, two men who were journeyman printers, and Mr. Leavenworth, the foreman.

All of them served, in one way or another, an iron beast that stood in the centre of the room. This beast was Mr. Mackenzie's printing-press, the first one Alec had ever seen close up.

Mr. Mackenzie's press had four iron legs, half like chair legs only with paws on them. It also had a broad iron forehead, which held things together at the top with two gold circles for eyes. Between the iron legs and the iron forehead were two iron jaws; when a journeyman had inked some type and covered it with paper, and when the pressman had cranked at the lower jaw and, by pulling a lever, brought the upper jaw down – squeeze! – the lower jaw came out again, the paper was pulled off the type, and there were printed words, black and shining wet, ready to be hung up to dry.

'Don't get your hand caught there, Master Alec,' said French. 'Why, we had a little apprentice boy in here – he slipped and fell right into the press and we printed him before we could stop ourselves – flat as a barn door.'

All along one wall were laid trays of type and in front of them was a table with a level stone top. Here the journeymen were setting up type from copy, hand-written on pieces of paper propped up in front of them. In their left hands, they held a composing stick; their right hands darted back and forth among the type boxes, ferreting out just the right letter. When their sticks – little metal boxes with handles – were squeezed full of type, they would transfer this from the stick to the stone table where the column of news or advertising they were setting was slowly being built up.

The type that was set up, tied together with string so it wouldn't fly apart, looked like a square pool of water to Alec. He loved the look of it. Mr. Mackenzie came up, put one hand on Alec's shoulder and one on the set-up type.

'There's freedom and liberty, lad. There's the mind of man. All his thoughts that thousands of people will read and find helpful – all these in thousands of wee bits of lead stuck together.'

Alec reached out and touched the set-up type. It was quite true. He was touching something that, when it was printed and published next Thursday in Mr. Mackenzie's paper, *The Colonial Advocate*, would be read all over Upper Canada and be part of people's minds forever.

'And here,' said Charley French, grinning, 'we have some pie. Care to have a slice?'

'I don't see any pie,' said Alec. All he saw was a boy of his own age, painfully sorting out some type he had spilled on the floor.

'That's the worst thing you can ever do, pie the type,' said French.

'How do you mean?'

'When you've spent hours setting something up – all of a sudden it goes – pie!'

After the type was set up and printed, it was brought back to the stone table, put back into the composing sticks ten lines at a time, and then put back, letter by letter, into the cases, each one of whose honeycomb-like cells lodged a single letter. The older journeymen could distribute the type so quickly that it sounded like rapid musket fire at a distance, when the soldiers were shooting down at the fort.

When you added all this up, and then put beside it the books and medicines that Mr. Mackenzie had for sale in the office, and the farmers coming in to deliver wood and apples as payment for their subscriptions; put beside it too Mr. Mackenzie coming in with more copy from his private office at the back, and the ships going in and out of the harbour, which you could see through the windows – the sum of it all was continual excitement.

Mr. Leavenworth now told French to take young Buchanan over to the case by the front door and teach him about quads, ems, ens, and all the rest of it.

'What are quads?' asked Alec.

'They're big spaces. Now, hold the stick this way, and I'll teach you more than spaces. I'll teach you A and great bouncing B all the way up to Z. But first you must learn to read your letters upside down. Here, I'll set you up a sentence of talk, and you see if you can read it.'

French nimbly filled the stick with letters from the case. Then Alec tried to read what French had set up.

Why are you so thin looking?

Doesn't Uncle John feed you?

'Why are you so thin looking? Doesn't Uncle John feed you?' tried Alec, reading the upside-down type. 'It was being up at the mill – they locked up the bread and cheese,' he replied. 'I'd have starved if I hadn't caught fish.'

'Good,' said French. 'Good, you can read stuff when

it's upside down. Bad, this miller starved you. Now I'll show you where the letters are in the case.' Alec soon mastered the following arrangement of the letters in the compartments of the type-case.

	)	(		k	j		e						$		1	2	3	4	5	6	7
	b	c		d					i		s	f	g		8	9	0	?	!		
															A	B	C	D	E	F	G
	l	m		n		h		o	y	p	,	w			H	I	K	L	M	N	O
z											q	;			P	Q	R	S	T	V	W
x	v	u		t				a		r	·	-			X	Y	Z			U	J

'These are the ones you gotta be careful of,' said French; 'b, d, p, and q all look alike – especially when they're upside down. If it looks like a q, it's a d. And if it's a p, it's really a b. So when I set up the word "bad" it looks upside down like pɐq – see?'

'No, I don't,' said Alec pressing his eyes with his hands.

'Oh, you will,' said French. 'Now – here's an advertisement for a lost cow. You try to set it up. And I'll come back in half an hour and see how you're getting on.'

Scribbled on a piece of paper was the following:

LOST: one sandy-coloured milk cow with white speckles.
Belonging to F. Shepard's farm up Yonge Street.

When French came by the first time, Alec had set this up as:

LATS: enos andy colcored mulch woth selkceps etwhi etc.

French roared with laughter. The next time he came by, Alec had set it up thusly:

LOST: one sandy-coloured F. Shephard with white speckles.
Belonging to Mr. Yonge on Cow Street.

But the next time French came by, Alec had it set up right, and from that moment on his progress in the skill of type-setting was, as Mr. Leavenworth put it, like a house on fire.

[7]

A SPOON FOR DOCTOR STRACHAN

ON a dark November night, a Saturday, Alec and Rebecca, the servant-girl, as the last of the household chores for that night, were sent out to bring in two pails of water. This they did; that is, they pumped the water and left it standing at the back door going down into the kitchen, but instead of going in immediately, they rather guiltily left Uncle John's property altogether and were soon proceeding quite swiftly down King Street in the direction of the English Church and that part of town where the Lieutenant-Governor and most of the wealthier people lived.

Rebecca wore a blue cloak with a hood and woollen gloves, the latter not just to cover the R on her right hand but to keep both hands warm, for it had lately turned bitterly cold.

Alec carried a huge nest, the crow's nest he had found in the woods; with the darkness, the nest looked, with its untidy twigs and reeds sticking out, a very mysterious object indeed – rather like a giant's wig or scalp.

Down King Street they walked beneath all the signs

– the Indian, the anvil, and the crowned boot; past the market and the stocks where bad people were sometimes put on public display; past the church, the court-house, and the jail.

There was going to be a ball that night at one of the hotels, and they could see servants lighting candles in the ballroom and others assisting a gentleman in decorating the dancing floor with a huge coat of arms made out of chalk and water colours. Two great lions faced each other across a shield that had not been finished as yet.

It was to be a masquerade ball and Lady Catherine sat at her looking-glass in Government House dressing herself as an Indian princess. She arranged wild birds' feathers in her hair. Sir Peregrine, her uncle, had shot their owners that autumn on the peninsula as they – the ducks – landed for a rest on their journey south. The cook had saved the prettier feathers for Lady Catherine. Reflected in a corner of her glass, she could see a cloaked figure and a boy in black homespun with a bird's nest in his hand.

'The mad youth who invited that pig in to tea and fetched poor Tully down from the Macalister roof. Hmph! Out bird-nesting in this weather. Oh, what folly!'

'Ahowrgh!' snarled Mr. Jarvis, dressed like the Black Huntsman, as he galloped suddenly out from a lane at them. But Mr. Jarvis's horse, nervous enough already with the Black Huntsman on its back, shied about a mile up in the air when he saw, or perhaps smelt, the crow's nest. With a positive cannonade of hooves, the frightened horse galloped off under a cursing Mr. Jarvis. Rebecca and Alec had no more trouble with him that night.

From a tavern with not very much of a door came the sound of fiddle music. They could see Charley French dancing a jig. He capered out to them, very drunkenly, and tried to pull them into the tavern, but neither Rebecca nor Alec cared to have a drop with him just then.

As they turned down Front Street it began to snow,

one large white flake at a time dancing out of the thick, inky murk above their heads. Alec pushed open the gate in the wall around Doctor Strachan's house. Rebecca drew back.

'I'm afraid, Master Alec.'

'Don't be afraid to claim your right, Rebecca. There can't be anything wrong with claiming your right.'

Doctor Strachan's coach dogs began to bark at them, and a servant opening the door told them to go around to the back. But Alec took Rebecca's hand and pushed his way through. He had caught sight of Doctor Strachan in his library and the thing to do was to march straight at him.

The learned doctor raised his head and gave both them and the nest such a stare that it almost pushed them right out of the room.

Rebecca turned away, but Alec got his mouth open and stammered, 'We've discovered the real thief of your silver, Doctor Strachan. Here's the silver pin. And you'll find the spoon at the bottom of the nest.' Very briefly he explained Croaker to the churchman.

Doctor Strachan did not say anything. The power of his stare weakened a bit, that was all. Alec had never seen anyone with such a sharp straight nose, such a determined mouth, and such strong-looking black hair. Doctor Strachan began to whistle under his breath, a rusty, tuneless, straw-vibrating, taste-souring whistle that made Alec shiver.

At length after an entire symphony of the winds, the churchman took the pin and examined it.

'Yes, lad, this is Mistress Strachan's.'

'What we want to know, sir, is – what about Rebecca's hand?'

'Well, what about it?'

'It shouldn't have been branded, sir. Her story was true, you see.'

Doctor Strachan stopped whistling.

'Take five pounds, girl?' he suddenly asked Rebecca. She would have said yes, but Alec cut in:

'Thirty pounds, Doctor. Thirty pounds and her young man can get out of debtor's jail, and they can get married. How'd you like to have capital R on your right hand for everyone to gawp at?'

'Oh sir,' wept Rebecca, 'if only my hand could be as it was before. That's all I – '

'That cannot be, you fool,' snapped Doctor Strachan. 'You're one of Mackenzie's apprentices, aren't you? I told John Macalister that was a mistake. Well, here – take your thirty pounds and get out. Rebecca, how at the time were we to know your daft story could be true?'

'But, sir, I thought God would tell a minister that I was speaking the truth. Did you not pray to him, Reverend Strachan?'

Strachan pressed a button that shot open a secret drawer in a rosewood desk. Out of this drawer he took money and very nearly threw it at them.

'And take that nest with you.'

'Oh no, sir,' said Alec. 'Your spoon's still in that nest. I left it in so you couldn't say we planted the things there. But I can feel it with my finger – here.'

Alec had put the nest on the floor. Doctor Strachan ran at the nest in a fury and began to kick it all over the room. The spoon soon flew out all right.

Alec and Rebecca also flew out the front door before he started in on them.

The snow was flying thick and fast now, and carriages were rolling towards the ball at the hotel. Alec left Rebecca at the jail where she was admitted to visit her sweetheart, a young farmer who since the harvest time had been imprisoned for debt by one of the tradesmen in the town. But the jailer would not let Alec go in, and so he walked over to Frank's Hotel where through a window he watched the dancers.

His favorite masquerader was Uncle John, who was attired as the Countess of Desmond, aged one hundred years. Young Raymond Baby, who, like Mr. Jarvis, was fond of riding down Mr. Mackenzie's apprentices, was dressed as Puss in Boots. Alec guessed who the Indian Princess was, and there was no difficulty at all in recognizing the Black Huntsman.

What a pretty, magic scene the ball seemed, now that his friend was happier. Alec looked and looked at the cedar-branched ceiling, the wreaths made of fir boughs, and the scores of tiny lights winking in their coloured-glass cups, winking and glittering from all sorts of unexpected places among the greenery. Later, as Alec turned away and started home for bed, he realized he must have been watching for quite a long time, because the shoes of the dancers had almost completely worn away what had earlier been painted and chalked on the ballroom floor – the two great lions and the shield they held between them.

[8]

ALEC'S JOURNAL

NEW YEAR'S DAY, 1826

YESTERDAY I bought this blank book from Mr. Mackenzie, who let me have it for a penny. He says that we should write down what happens to you, or else you will forget the life you have lived. And that would be to live like a dog or a cat. I am sitting by the fire in Uncle John's kitchen writing this. The wind is howling a terrible blizzard of snow outside. Charley French helped me take proofs of all the picture cuts Mr. Mackenzie has in his office to make his paper pretty with, and I can paste them from time to time in this book.

Now this is a very fearsome picture of a lion's head. They put it in the paper when they are advertising an apprentice boy who has run away from his master –

as one-eyed Clem did from Mr. Douro, the hat-maker on King Street. I guess it's to frighten him back when he sees it in the paper.

I don't think I shall run away again now.

Allan called me Reverend again today in the passageway. I gave him some of my butternuts to crack and eat, hoping he would be softened to me, but I don't think it's going to work.

JANUARY 6

This is the day the Wise Men came to see Jesus. I remember Father telling us that. The snow has packed down enough so that the farmers can come into market again with their sleighs. I love to hear their bells ringing on the horses' harness. They cover themselves up with buffalo robes, and the sight of these brings back the Red River country very strongly to me.

The wolves can be heard howling in the forest at night. And a deer ran through the town this morning. Mr. Hagerman's cow fell into the drinking-hole his cowman had cut for her in the harbour. All of us apprentices sallied out to help get her onto the ice again.

FEBRUARY 28

I melted some old cast-away type down in an iron ladle at the fire and made myself five lead soldiers. I made the mould for them out of clay I got in the garden when it thawed. Some of Cousin Bathsheba's plants are still hardy and green under the snow, when everything else in the garden has been frozen dead since October.

Joel, who now sleeps in Master Allan's room, says that when Uncle John asks me to tell him what Mr. Mackenzie is going to print in his paper on Thursday I should. But I say that I should not.

Mr. Mackenzie has criticized the government very harshly lately. Uncle John is in charge of spending the taxes that the people pay in, but the people, says Mr. Mackenzie, have no control over how Uncle John and Sir Peregrine, the Lieutenant-Governor, decide to spend it. I used to think that Uncle John kept the tax money in the house somewhere, and perhaps I should stumble upon it some day – a great mass of gold, or would it be silver? But now Aunt Henrietta tells me it is kept in the Bank of Upper Canada, not far down the street.

Yesterday the apprentice boys had a snowball fight with the scholars at the Blue School. The old stumps that stand about the common near there and the ravine with the little bridge across it are almost perfect for a really good snowball war.

Afterwards, some of us tangled with the law students who study just around the corner from our printing-shop. We knocked off two hats. Here is a picture of a hat such as gentlemen must wear. I hope I need never wear one.

MARCH 21

It is still very cold. The ice is glassy and crystal clear all over the harbour. Everyone has been out skating. I saw an Indian trapper yesterday and his family. They went to meet him, he on his snowshoes coming up out of the marsh at the mouth of the river. I like to think of him disappearing on a snowy day as he goes around his trap line. He sees so many things while we are cooped up in our stuffy rooms.

Sometimes when the boys are let out to play, I stay behind and ask to read one of the books in the shop. I am half way through Don Quixote.

They say that Doctor Strachan who is the Rector of this town has left to go to Quebec. How I should like to go down the road to Quebec. It's very funny, but you notice the difference when he is away. He is so strong. Uncle John very likely thinks he is the strongest person in the town now.

> I'm the king of the castle!
> Get down, you dirty rascal!

APRIL I

Joel warned me not to try any April Fool tricks on Uncle John, or anybody else, as I usually do.

APRIL 20

The ships have come to the harbour for the ice is gone. The wild geese went over again last night. At night you can see the torches of the men out spearing the salmon in the lake as they come in to the river mouth.

Mr. Jarvis splashed me with mud today by galloping at me. Even he calls me Reverend. I wonder if I could save up enough money to get a horse. I usually get to work through all the mud by working my way along the fences like Lady Catherine's monkey. Whenever there is a lost horse or mare Mr. Leavenworth

has this picture put in the paper. I think this horse would not splash me.

MAY I

Uncle John has had printed at the other printing office a little book attacking Mr. Mackenzie. I guess he is angry because Mr. Mackenzie is always printing about how Uncle John and his friends govern Upper Canada for themselves and not for the good of the people.

Uncle John in his little book laughs at Mr. Mackenzie's old mother who lives with him. Uncle John had it printed that the only reason he, Uncle John, subscribed to the *Colonial Advocate*, Mr. Mackenzie's paper, was to help support that poor old lady. What an odd sense of humour Uncle John has.

What Uncle John does not know is that we are setting up right now the funniest reply that Mr.

Mackenzie is writing to Uncle John's book. This will bring him down a peg or two.

Tomorrow I am to go with Charley French in a wagon to Ancaster and back, and all the subscribers have been warned to pay up if they see us and that we will be going by.

The apple trees are just about to come out in the garden here. Perhaps we'll meet the stage-coach to-morrow – a stage-coach like this. How long the coach-

man's whip is – I think I will just continue it with my pen like this – now I must go to bed, the candle's nearly out.

[9]

A VERY SHORT CHAPTER

ONE evening in late May, Alec had just come
back from the classes he attended at the
house of Mr. Lang, the schoolmaster, and was
about to read the servants a particularly thrilling
chapter from *The Last of the Mohicans* – a part where
cannon-balls were whizzing through the mist in front
of an old fort and where there were promising signs
of an Indian massacre later on. Just at this moment,
Joel came to the head of the kitchen stairs and called
Alec to come up.

'Do I have to come?' groaned Alec. Since neither
Rebecca nor any of the other servants could read and
he could, Alec felt this interruption very keenly.

He did have to come.

Up in the drawing-room, white candles were gleaming, each with a gold sparkling flame. The family had
been playing cards and the gold clock on the mantel
chimed half past nine.

'Alec Buchanan,' said his uncle, putting down his
cards, 'this may be your last chance. If you don't
tell me what Mackenzie's going to print in his paper
next Thursday, I may have to send you up to the

66

mill again. And Mr. Jakes is up there alone right now.'

'Uncle John, why do you want to know what Mr. Mackenzie's going to publish next Thursday? Can't you wait and see?'

'Perhaps, Alec, if the Government were to know beforehand, they would say that he shouldn't publish it – on Thursday, or any other day.'

'I guess that's why those people in Ancaster dressed up that scarecrow, stuck your name on it, and hanged it in front of the tavern. You're no friend of a free press.'

'Why, John,' said Aunt Henrietta, 'you never told me the rascals had done this.'

Uncle John's face went white, then red, and finally with great effort went back to its normal Uncle-John colour. Alec was thinking of the quickest way to get back to *The Last of the Mohicans*. Why not tell Uncle John?

'So you want to go back to the mill?'

'No. I doubt you could send me, Uncle John. Am I not Mr. Mackenzie's apprentice?'

'Oh, I might change that.' Uncle John paused while this sank in. 'So, will you tell me?'

'Yes.'

'Good boy. I knew you'd come round to seeing the interests of our class. I'd always hoped you'd side with the Loyalists. It might be very useful to have a little Loyalist in that den of republicanism. A little Loyalist.'

'You really want me to tell you some of the things Mr. Mackenzie is going to say in his paper on Thursday?'

'Yes, Alec. Only there's no need to call him Mr. Mackenzie. Just call him Mackenzie.'

'Well, Uncle John,' said Alec looking up at the chandelier, 'he's going to publish a long piece of printing where he says what a bunch of snobs the governing class are here. They've grabbed up a lot of the best land and never do anything with it. You won't let the soldiers go to the church they want to go to; they must go to your church or not at all.'

'I see,' said Uncle John, drumming his fingers on the table. 'What else does he say?'

'He says that the Honourable Mr. Robbins, or is it Bobbins, who carries his head so high and has such a great coat of arms on his great big coach – why his father was naught but a New York shoemaker back before the American rebellion and before he fled up here.'

'Go on.'

'Must I?'

'Don't stop now.'

'He says, Uncle John, that your father was just a farrier in the army, for all you keep saying he was a distinguished surgeon. He took excellent care of Governor Simcoe's horses and so – '

'Oh!' roared Uncle John.

'Now, John,' put in Aunt Henrietta, 'you did ask the boy to tell you what's being printed.'

'I didn't say it,' protested Alec getting ready to escape. 'You'll see it in Thursday's paper. Extra copies on request, Uncle John.'

'Get out of here,' roared Uncle John. 'Get out of here! Get out of my sight, you insolent young puppy!'

Uncle John began to roar that Alec must have told Mackenzie that his father was a horse doctor. Alec said no, he didn't have to. Everyone in York knew that Uncle John's father had started out as a farrier. It was common knowledge. Hereupon, Uncle John took up a poker and chased Alec right out of the house.

He didn't catch Alec, but he forbade him the house.

From that evening on Alec slept in a loft above the stables, no great misery since the weather had turned warm and summery, and Rebecca brought him out lots of food. The reading of *The Last of the Mohicans* still went on, this time in the harness room. Since there were still ugly rumours that Mr. Jakes was coming down to get him, Alec now began to feel that it really did not matter whether he obeyed Uncle John or not.

〖 10 〗

A PIE FOR SUNDAY

THE first Sunday in June was a happy blue and green day, the morning part of which Alec spent in walking about the town and watching the people.

The streets were in a pleasant state in which they were neither muddy nor yet dusty, and down them at church time came a procession of coaches and gigs filled with the patrician families who attended the English Church. Alec's eyes were dazzled by the uniforms of the servants, the coats of arms on the sides of the coaches, the dress of the ladies, the dark-blue, gold-buttoned coats of the gentlemen. Dazzling to both eye and ear were the soldiers who marched up from the fort in their red coats, white trousers, and tall indescribable caps – all to the tune of their own band. Doctor Strachan's coach, surmounted by a large gilded globe, minus the Doctor though, who was still in Quebec, now came rattling up and the band music closed as the soldiers filed into the church through their special door. The last people into the church were an old couple who walked in from their farm on the river flats – an old colonel and his wife, who still

wore the fashions of fifty years ago, wig, three-cornered hat, long waistcoat, kerchief, and all.

As Alec drifted away in the warm sunlight, he could hear the bassoon playing in the church, deep underneath the singing, and from other chapels and churches came singing – singing that would suddenly stop, then, as you got farther away from it, resume in a distant buzzing way.

There were Indians encamped in the market-place. One of them in red leggings and white blanket stood smoking a morning pipe in front of his tent. In a muddy place, a large sow and her shoats lay asleep in the sun; the air, however, was filled with bees and other insects that were off on buzzing journeys of their own and knew neither Sunday nor rest while the sun shone. Alec felt very lonely. Before dinner, which

he ate by himself at Uncle John's order, he sat out the
rest of the morning by Bathsheba's garden and plan-
ned improvements he might make tomorrow, for since
it was the Sabbath he was afraid to do anything that
could be called work. Some of her plants had survived
the winter, and he had planted the seeds of others
gathered and kept last fall. But nothing had come up
as yet.

The shadows of Sunday at noon shortened until they stood right under you. After dinner, they would come out on the other side of you.

Some hours later, Alec was sitting with his back to one of the Macalister pear trees. Like lingering snowflakes, white blossom petals still lay about on the grass where Alec was reading his pocket Bible.

He could see Joel slouching idly about the side of the house by the beehives, as if he were trying to make up his mind about something.

'What is it, Jo?' Joel started to come to him and soon stood looking down at him. 'I hardly see you any more, Joel. What have you been up to?'

'Busy with Uncle John.'

'Heavens! Do you even work in his office on Sundays? I saw you there with Allan this morning.'

'Oh. It was something Uncle John sent us to look up.'

'Joel,' said Alec, after calmly surveying his brother's face for a few seconds. 'Allan said a very funny thing to me yesterday. He said, "Reverend, if we don't beat you apprentice boys one way we'll starve you out another." What does he mean – "starve us out"?'

'Bless my soul if I know,' said Joel.

' "Bless my soul" – that's the way the Grammar School boys talk. I think you've become a Tory, Joel.'

'Maybe. I want to be a gentleman when I grow up.'

'Same thing.'

'Alec, there's a question I wanted to ask you. When is Mr. Mackenzie coming back to town?'

'How did you know he was away?'

'I saw him go by in the stage-coach on Friday.'

'He's gone down to Queenston, but I really don't know when he'll be back.'

'Why'd he go to Queenston?'

'He wants to raise some money there. What do you want to know for?'

'Oh, I just wondered after seeing him get on the stage-coach. Say, he certainly won't be back today if he's gone to Queenston by stage-coach. He won't even be there yet.'

'No,' said Alec. 'Joel, why don't we borrow Charley French's skiff and go over to the lighthouse?'

'Haven't the time, Reverend,' came Joel's voice from the top of the garden where he had already withdrawn. Then he disappeared.

Some minutes later, a hand opened the bull's-eye

window in the gable of Uncle John's house and waved a handkerchief back and forth three times.

Half an hour later, lulled by the summer heat and the bees buzzing in the lilac bushes, Alec fell asleep. He slept for some hours during which he had a curious dream that his father had come to the other side of a river and was signalling to him. When he asked the ferryman to row him across to his father, he caught sight of Joel smirking and shaking his head. The ferryman had no ears and both of his hands were branded with letters. When the boat crossed the river, it knocked against the bank in a funny, chattery manner – bumpity, bumpity. The ferryman was making his boat do that so Alec could not get from the boat to his father, who stretched out his hands to help him.

'Wake up, Master Alec. Wake up,' cried Rebecca. The bumping of the boat was her shaking him, and the ferryman's marked hands faded into her one marked hand.

'What is it, Rebecca?' Alec rubbed his eyes and started at how much longer the shadows were.

'The Tory boys are setting to march on Mr. Mackenzie's place and tear it down or something bad like that.'

'We must run to one of the magistrates. There's Mr. Allan, he's a magistrate and lives right close.'

'Master Alec, I have run to him and he says he won't come. He says he's got no call to defend upstart disloyal people's property.'

'How do you know they're going to do anything to Mr. Mackenzie's house, Rebecca?'

Rebecca explained that she had been out walking along Palace Street by the lake front and thinking of her young man, who not twenty miles away was probably walking about his newly-sown farm thinking of her. Peter would have walked in to see her that Sunday, but to take a journey on Sunday was forbidden in their Bible, even to see a loved one. Perhaps he would come in next market day.

Happening to glance back at her employer's house, she had seen someone signalling with a handkerchief from the round window in the gable.

'It was Master Joel, Alec,' said Rebecca. 'I saw his face in the window.'

Rebecca had then turned to see whom he might be signalling to. She caught sight of Mr. Jarvis stepping under the Merchants' Wharf. By walking out on the wharf as others were doing in promenade fashion and by straining her ears, she was just able to hear Jarvis say to someone else under the wharf that 'the Scotsman certainly wouldn't be back today . . . meet at the place where the cudgels . . . set up some type for the Scotsman.'

Alec told Rebecca to run to Snyder's Tavern and find Charley French.

'Tell him to get down to the shop on the double,' said Alec, as he himself ran out of the garden and tore down the street towards the printing-shop.

King Street was deserted. Any people who were abroad were down at the wharf watching a steamboat depart, and there were not many of these, for it was the time of day when most families in York were having tea or supper. The tin trumpet sounded from the boat, the signal that the *Martha Ogden* was about to leave.

Alec hammered at the Mackenzie house door. It seemed ages before Mr. Mackenzie's old mother came down to answer. Both she and Mr. Mackenzie's oldest boy, James, an apprentice to the printing trade like Alec, wondered what Alec was so excited about on such a calm Sunday evening. Old Mrs. Mackenzie had a cup of tea in her hand.

'The Tory boys are coming to wreck the shop.

We've got to try and stop them. Rebecca says she can't get Mr. Allan to stir. James, you go over and tell him. I'm too small. Surely he won't stand by and watch a man's house get broken into.'

While James, who really had the red hair that was represented in his father by a red wig, flew over to Mr. Allan's house, Alec tried to push some of the heavy tables up against the front door. James came back with the same news Rebecca had. Magistrate Allan could not be bothered, although he now emerged from his house to watch whatever needed watching. Needless to say, Mr. Allan was of the Government party.

'They're singing,' said James. They could hear quite a few voices singing something like

> 'Since he prints tripe,
> We'll smash his type.
> All for King and Country.'

'They've each one got a big stick,' said James.

About twelve young men and youths headed by Mr. Jarvis came up from beneath the bank onto Palace Street, marching in single file. They came straight towards the door of the printing office, and James hurried both Alec and his grandmother out of the place for fear they would be hurt.

The rioters acted as if there were nothing more legal or worthy to do on a Sunday evening than to smash up the press and type of a newspaper that had dared to criticize their fathers and poke fun; had dared to say that Grandfather, instead of being a noble lord, had been a humble cobbler in the army. Underneath

the lampblack some of the attackers had daubed on
their faces, Alec easily recognized Cousin Allan, John
Lyons, who was the Lieutenant-Governor's private
secretary, quite a few law students from Uncle John's
office and the offices of other prominent officials, and
Raymond Baby and his brother Charles.

Their leader pushed open the door, the rioters filed
into the shop, and soon the sounds of smashing and
throwing drifted out.

Alec looked over at Magistrate Allan, who was grinning and laughing with the rioters.

'What a shame this is!' cried James to Mr. Jarvis. 'What a shame to wreck a man's livelihood.'

'You say a word,' blustered out Jarvis, his face reddening under the lampblack, 'and I'll knock you down.'

With hammer and sticks, the Tory boys soon finished pounding the type that was set up. Then they pied it by sweeping it onto the floor. Six of them heaved at the press until they had toppled it over. It went over with a tremendous big crash, heard up and down the street. Some passers-by stopped to watch, and one of them, a carpenter, would have helped if he had not seen Mr. Allan standing by. What could he, one man, do against a dozen men? Why should he move when the law itself did not move? Even Charley French, when he came running up, and he was more reckless than most, decided watching was best.

The quoins and leads were smashed and bent. The composing stone was pushed over and cracked. The

picture cuts were mutilated with nails like this – and last of all each one of the rioters seized a tray of type and came outside with it. Some chose to dump their tray in Mr. Mackenzie's garden. Others raced down to the wharf and threw the cases into the lake.

'Well done, boys!' cheered Mr. Allan as they filed off again, leaving the door of the printing-shop open behind them. Alec could hear a familiar voice laughing under the bank. While James comforted his grandmother, who was weeping and very disturbed, Alec watched the Tory boys leave their cudgels at his uncle's office and then disperse, laughing and joking, in great high spirits.

He went down to the lake to wash off the lampblack that Cousin Allan had smeared on his cheeks as a parting gesture. In the water he saw something gleaming. It was a great capital letter R that had fallen out of the cases thrown into the lake by the rioters.

He picked it up and turned about. The swallows

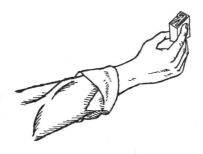

were flitting back and forth from their nests under the wharf. He caught sight of his uncle sneaking down the beach, hugging the shadows of the bank and thinking, no doubt, that no one saw him. Alec put the capital letter R in his pocket.

〖 11 〗

AN UNEXPECTED RETURN

WHICH one of you lads,' said Mr. Mackenzie coming out from his office where he thought out and wrote things, 'will take this message down to the wharf and hand it to Sir Peregrine, the Lieutenant-Governor, as he gets on the boat?'

'I'll take it, sir,' said Charley French, pushing forward first. All of the apprentices were engaged in sorting out type, and separating the damaged from the undamaged. The day before had been spent in finding the type, which had been sprinkled about the premises like lead snow. They raised their heads now to watch Charley run down to the wharf, where the Lieutenant-Governor's coach was being rolled onto the boat. Sir Peregrine was going away for the summer to his other house across the lake on the Niagara Peninsula.

'Sir Peregrine has shown no sign of having heard about the type riot here,' explained Mr. Mackenzie. 'And if he gets away from us he may never hear about it.'

'What will happen if he's told?' asked Alec.

'Why, he'll have to tell the Attorney-General to lay charges against the rioters. I've put a list of the rioters' names and witnesses' names in that packet, and some pieces of broken type. I dare him to ignore that.'

But in a few minutes Charley French came back with the packet and explained that the soldiers had blocked his way.

'You should have told them,' growled Mr. Mackenzie, and Charley French visibly quailed at the look in his employer's eye, 'that it's the business of a ruler to receive a subject's petition. Come! Billy Doyle! See what you can do. You'll have to run right up on the boat now to catch hold of him.'

Billy Doyle, a rather fat apprentice whose cheeks were so chubby they wobbled when he ran, now gal-

loped with the message for Sir Peregrine. But the captain of the ship, who was excessively proud of carrying the Lieutenant-Governor on his boat – so proud that he had just raised a special flag in his honour, and also, until a few hours ago, had refused to take on any other passengers – turned Billy Doyle back at the gang-plank.

'Do I have to go myself?' roared Mr. Mackenzie, taking off his wig and slapping it back on.

'I'll get it to him,' chimed Alec, who as the smallest apprentice had thought it better to hang back.

The ship's trumpet was being blown and the regimental band was playing a farewell tune; so Alec knew he must act quickly. After wriggling his way through a knot of officials, he got onto the boat by buying a one-way ticket, deck passage, to Queenston. That took his life savings.

Once on the boat, however, there were still difficulties, for Sir Peregrine, Lady Maitland, and Lady Catherine sat inside their coach. It sat on the deck, and the deck all about the coach had been roped off and was guarded by flunkeys. Alec began to wonder if he might not have to walk back when he got across to Queenston, for the boat would soon sail.

But an old friend was sitting on top of the viceregal coach – Tully, Lady Catherine's pet monkey. Alec took two butternuts out of his pantaloon pocket and, holding the packet under one arm, knocked the butternuts together in a way that used to bring half a dozen squirrels flocking up in the forest around Uncle John's mill. All sound on wharf and boat ceased, or seemed to, while Alec made the peculiar clicking sound.

In the silence, the monkey leaped off the coach and streaked over to Alec, eager for a butternut.

'Hullo, Tully,' said Alec, looking into the creature's mournful eyes. 'If you take this to Sir Peregrine you can have one of these.'

The monkey scuttled back and forth with the utmost understanding and dispatch. Sir Peregrine had the envelope, Tully had a butternut, and Alec was on the gang-plank, all simultaneously.

'I don't think I'll be going to Queenston after all,' said Alec to the ticket man. 'Could I have my money back?'

'Here, Tully,' cooed Lady Catherine. 'Let me give you a proper English filbert instead of that nasty native nut. I'm sure you'll break all your teeth on it.'

'The fools!' muttered Sir Peregrine. He looked at a piece of broken type through his eye-glass. Then, after glancing down the list of names in Mr. Mackenzie's message, he beckoned to his private secretary, Mr. Lyons, and whispered something to the young man that made the latter change colour.

Right after Alec came off, Lyons also tramped off with his baggage. He had just been fired from his job for taking part in the type riot.

'And so I must give up all notion of getting away from this wretched hole during the entire summer!' cried the young man, flinging his hat down on the wharf.

The boat now began to move away, and from the fort, cannon boomed out and white puffs of smoke floated up.

'I'll get you for this,' growled Uncle John, squeezing Alec's shoulder. 'I'll get you.'

'I suppose you will, Uncle John,' said Alec walking up to Palace Street as in a dream.

'Good work, lad,' laughed Mr. Mackenzie when Alec came back to the shop, mission accomplished. It was the first time the printer had laughed since re-

turning from Queenston a night or two ago to find his
press overturned.

So far as Alec was concerned, whatever might occur
was worth that laughter.

'What's under that sacking?' asked Joel, looking up
at his uncle's eyes across a wagon he had found standing in front of the house at dinner time.

Uncle John cleared his throat and murmured that
it was a calf he was sending up to the mill to be
fattened for the slaughter. Just at this moment, Mr.
Jakes, Uncle John's bailiff and man of all trades, came
out of the courtyard with a team of horses and began
to hitch them up to the wagon.

'Joel,' said his uncle with softness. 'Joel. I thought

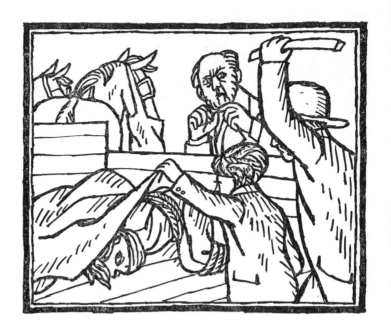

we understood each other so well on Sunday. If you
want to grow up to be a gentleman, do not lift that
sacking. Take my word for it. It is painful, but it has
to be done.'

Joel's hands shook as he snatched back the pile of
sacks that covered something on the floor of the
wagon. It was Alec tied hand and foot with a white
handkerchief stuffed in his mouth.

'Oh, *what* has to be done!' blurted out Joel, forgetting himself completely. 'My brother to be treated
like a beast!' He snatched the cloth out of Alec's
mouth. 'No, I don't want to grow up to be a gentleman if you're one, Uncle. Help me untie him this
instant!'

'Why, of course!' said Uncle John, reaching forward
to undo a knot, but secretly motioning to the burly

figure who was now walking up the wagon tongue and so behind Joel's back. 'I see it now. It is a wretched mistake on my part to punish the boy so severely. Ah – uh – '

Sparks flew up into Joel's eyes as Jakes cuffed him from behind, and Uncle John tipped him into the wagon beside his brother. Uncle John's face, his house with its windows, the bull's-eye window, and the chimneys spun around and around until Joel couldn't remember any more.

'Cover them both up, Jakes. Keep 'em warm. I hope the larger one enjoys shovelling grain this afternoon and I'll ride up this evening to see how things are getting on.'

'Aye, sir. Aye,' said Jakes, picking up the lines. Uncle John watched the wagon move away and then disappeared into his elegant house.

Joel came to after they had passed through the toll-gate and just as they were rumbling over the bridge. He shook his head clear and immediately began to work at the fastenings that still held Alec. But they were wheeling down the forest road before Alec was free. The deep, dark-green shade of the countless leaves hid the sun.

At the buttonwood tree that leaned over the road, Mr. Jakes whoaed the horses and reached up into the low-hanging branch for an object he had hidden there – a pistol.

'You get up here and hold the lines, since you're so smart at undoing things,' he yelled at Alec. Alec crawled up to the front of the wagon and was made to hold the reins. Jakes came back and sat opposite Joel.

'Get a move on there! Get a move on!'

'I've not driven horses for a long time,' croaked Alec, who was still recovering from the gagging he had suffered earlier.

'Well, try to remember!' bawled Jakes, 'or I'll shoot your big brother here.' The horses began to move, and with a quick-beating heart Alec watched the forest slide by. As soon as the road widened into the mill yard, and it was even widening now, he knew there would be a scene even more violent than the preceding ones.

'Whoa!' shouted Jakes. He slid off the wagon and motioned to the boys that they were to get down. 'For I want to tie one of you to the mill-wheel and I need the other to help me.'

'How on earth did you lose your ears?' asked Alec quietly.

'What?!' The brute roared so that the mill yard echoed.

'Pray watch out behind you, Mr. Jakes,' continued Alec. A huge bear had just come up from the river where it had been fishing. It was looking at the boys and the wagon, but its front paws were placed on Mr. Jakes's wide, enormous shoulders.

At the entrance to the harbour, from the top of the lighthouse, a blue flag unfurled and straightened out in the fresh lake breeze. By this, the harbourmaster knew that the *Frontenac* would soon be steaming in from Kingston.

From the steamer, after it had docked at the Merchants' Wharf, there alighted two passengers in particular: first a young girl, her face ever so slightly dusted with freckles; second, a young-looking man, bearded, curiously dressed, half in skins, half in homespun, his face sunburnt as if he had lately been as much in the open as the Indians continually were. Putting the girl's trunk on his shoulder, both man and girl, laughing and talking, proceeded in the direction of Uncle John's house.

'Why would the boys run off?' asked Mr. Mackenzie of Uncle John. He was standing in front of the latter's house, whither he had come on a sudden suspicion that Alec's absence from work was unusual.

'Well, I'm sure I don't know,' said Uncle John.

'That is why I was just on my way to your printing-shop to get a notice printed, "Lost: two nephews." When they don't come home for dinner, and you say my younger nephew isn't at your shop, I can only conclude they've run off.'

'I'll print no such sign for you.'

'Of course, Mackenzie. I had forgot. You've had a riot at your place, haven't you. I understand that during both our absences from town, some jolly prankster came and upset a few galleys of type for you. That is a pity.'

'Why is it a pity, Macalister, if I may be so bold as to ask?'

'Because it will damage your livelihood, and you may not be able to support your dear old mother any longer.'

Quite pardonably, Mr. Mackenzie took off his wig, slapped it back on and raised his fist.

'Here, here,' came a pleasant voice from the traveller aforementioned. 'Don't strike my brother-in-law. If he's done anything naughty, I'm quite sure he'll see the error of his ways if we reason with him.'

'Father,' said Bathsheba, 'can you guess who this is? Where are the Buchanan boys? I want to see their faces when they find out that I have come back with their father.'

'But,' gasped Uncle John, 'the boys – the boys told me you'd died, Rob.'

'I expect they did. Everyone at Red River thought I had been killed by savage Indians. And so I very nearly was. But I escaped into the wilderness and made my way to Hudson Bay, where one boat took me to live with the Moravian missionaries in Labrador, and another boat brought me to Montreal where I took ship with your Bathsheba. I happened to see her name in the *Frontenac*'s passenger list, and I immediately sought her out to see if she knew anything of my lost sons. They have come to you, John. How kind of you to protect them for me. Where are they?'

'Why, whatever is the matter, Father?' inquired Bathsheba.

'Well, there they are,' said Uncle John. After a preliminary rattling and rumbling, a wagon bearing both boys and guided by Alec appeared around the corner and bore down on the group of onlookers in such a determined way that they retired for safety's sake into Uncle John's garden.

We left the boys at the mill. What had happened was this – the bear had been fishing, but it caressed Jakes in such a close way that it might be said to be about, not to fish, but to man.

Alec pulled at the lines and turned the horses back towards town.

'Hey, boys,' quavered Mr. Jakes, breaking out of the bear's grasp. 'Hey, wait up, boys! What's the big hurry? Sure we'll go back into town. Let's go back into town, boys, and talk it over with your Uncle John. I only meant to cuff you a bit and scare you. I didn't mean to tie you to the wheel, oh boys, this bear is going to eat me up – awhrgh!'

Alec's response to this was to slap the lines down hard on the horses' backs, and all the way back to town he never let them slow down. So the three parties kept about an equal distance from each other: first, boys and wagon; then Mr. Jakes, who ran off a great deal of fat that day and lost his pistol into the bargain; last of all the bear. The bear growled just often enough to keep Mr. Jakes closer to the wagon than to the bear. But Alec drove the wagon just fast enough that Mr. Jakes never quite caught up with it.

After crossing the bridge, they ran through the toll-gate without paying toll, so that the toll-gate keeper and his daughter can now be added to the procession that hurtled, screamed, lumbered, and waddled towards Uncle John's front gate.

'There's Father!' shouted Alec, jumping down from the wagon and running towards the man dressed in skins. Joel jumped down too and the horses ran off down to King Street, which they crossed somewhat unexpectedly (a horseman or two fell off their horses as a result) with Mr. Jakes still in pursuit, and also the toll-gate keeper still calling for a general hue and cry. But the bear saw better game in Uncle John's bee-hives and loped off into the garden to sample their contents once again, for this was the same bear that Alec had loosed from Mr. Gosling's yard in the spring.

'Why, boys,' said their father after he had hugged each of them several times, 'what is this I hear about your running away? And now I see you come running back. Has Uncle John not been good to you?'

'Not been good to us!' exclaimed Alec. Both Alec and Joel told their father of Uncle John's latest kindness to them.

'Brother John,' said their father when his children

had finished. There was a light in his eyes that was even scarier than the light that came into Mr. Mackenzie's eyes on first hearing of the type riot. 'How could you have the nerve to do this to my children when not only would they – *must* they – have brought enough money with them from the Red River country to pay for their schooling, but – why, you still owe my father the thousand pounds he lent your father to start up in business here!'

Uncle John obviously had no answer to this. Bathsheba stretched out her hand to him, but he brushed it angrily away. Just then a bee stung him, one of those disturbed by the bear, and with a yell of rage he ran into his house and shut the door.

Their father laughed.

'We shall have to go into his house and reason with him some more. Bathsheba, you go in and tell him I should like to speak with him alone. After a while. But I should like to talk to my boys first, as we walk up and down this garden.'

Bathsheba went into the house, and the boys and their father, after parting with Mr. Mackenzie, walked farther into the garden over the gravelled paths.

What a lot they had to tell each other! The boys told of journeys up rushing, dark, northern rivers edged with unknown forests, and finally, a descent into a place of houses and poplar trees, trees planted by hand, where the brothers had almost been divided from each other.

The father told of escape from the murderous heathen, of pitting himself against desolate, trackless wastes, of seeing the wilderness empty as birds fled south at winter's approach and of seeing the animals that remained turn white so that both hunter and hunted might not be seen against the snow. But the spring, and a ship going south and then up the great river that flows out of Canada, had brought the father back to his sons, just at the time when the sons had been brought back to each other.

When their father had finished the tale of his travels they were silent, watching the shadow on the sun-dial that stood in the centre of the garden. Then the Reverend Mr. Buchanan looked at Alec's clothes, which were the same homespun black as he had been wearing on the steamboat nearly a year ago.

'We must get you some new things to wear, Alec. You need not wear mourning for your father any more. Nor for any other reason either.'

[12]

HUZZAH!

THE courtroom was packed on the Indian summer afternoon when Mr. Mackenzie's suit for damages against the type rioters was to be decided – for or against. The lion and the unicorn on the coat of arms above the judge's chair looked down at the people, and Alec looked back at them. Lady Catherine occasionally waved a pink and gilt fan back and forth, but only occasionally, since there had been cold weather recently, and although it was now warm outside, the courtroom itself was still rather chilly and damp.

At last the jury entered. Some of the older jurymen looked rather pale. It was later learned they had sat up all night arguing with one stubborn man who had wanted to award Mackenzie damages of only one hundred and fifty pounds. The foreman stood up and everyone was quiet.

'Your lordship,' said the foreman, 'we the jury conclude that the type rioters, Mr. Jarvis and the others, should be fined for their outrageous act, and the money given over to Mr. Mackenzie to restore his printing-shop completely as it was before the riot. The fine they must pay is six hundred and twenty-five pounds sterling.'

Three-quarters of the audience cheered at this. One-quarter groaned, for they were the relatives and parents who would have to pay for their offspring's prank.

When Alec and Joel first came to York the authorities were hanging a poor man for killing a cow. When they left York, a year later, a dozen or so idle young men were being fined, albeit a huge fine, but still only being fined, for wrecking an expensive and complicated printing-shop, worth a hundred cows, a shop out of which almost a dozen people made their living.

'When they left York' – they were leaving that very afternoon for Scotland, where the Reverend Mr. Buchanan had fallen heir to his father's land. The steamer *Frontenac* was sailing for Kingston at four and their luggage was already aboard.

The judge finished speaking, the court rose, and a confused hubbub of voices broke out.

'I shall have to sell my horse,' sulked Master Raymond Baby.

'This country is relapsing into barbarism,' said Lady Catherine. 'I'm sure the young gentlemen cannot do anything to entertain themselves, the tradesmen are so particular about the law.'

'How will I pay for my seven new waistcoats?' moaned another young rioter. 'With all that money, Mackenzie's apprentices will dress up better than we do.'

At the door of the court-house the apprentices stood waiting for their employer. When he appeared they

gave him a loud and hearty cheer, a sound that made those calling for their coaches wince and look sour, but made most of those proceeding on foot smile.

'Huzzah! Huzzah! for Mackenzie and Liberty!'

'Mackenzie! and Freedom of the Press!'

'Are you sad to leave York?' said the boys' father as, later on, the Macalister coach trundled them about in a farewell tour of the town.

The boys could not make up their minds.

'It's an odd little place. Already it has its poor quarter and its rich quarter, its jail and its church. And yet you would think in the New World we could get away from the evil old ways. You would almost think there was no other way to arrange human beings. What are those curiously painted posts I keep seeing about the town?'

Their father pointed to a smooth pale-blue post, round as a pillar, with a wooden globe on top painted white.

'That's the limit post for the debtors in the jail,' explained Joel. 'When they're let out for their daily walk they must go no farther than this post in this direction, or else forfeit all their privileges back at the jail.'

'I suppose,' mused their father, 'when I was walking to Hudson Bay I would have wept to see a white and blue post that meant I need walk no farther. But here it makes me grind my teeth at the traps people set for each other.'

Alec observed that there were Indians encamped again at the market-place. The soldiers in their red coats were marching to a drum at the fort. The Union Jack waved in the autumn haze. Some pigs that had been lying in the middle of the road enjoying the mud squealed as the coachman flicked them out of the way with his whip.

At the wharf their friends were present to say farewell. Aunt Henrietta, Bathsheba, and Cousin Allan came down with them in the coach, having joined them near the end of their tour of the town. Uncle John, Mr. Jakes, and the bear, for one reason or another, did not show up.

'You must excuse my father not being here,' said Bathsheba, putting her hand on Alec's shoulder. 'He is feeling out of sorts with himself. If I had been here I would have tried to soften his harshness. But it's all past now. Or is it?'

'It's all past,' said Alec. 'I don't feel a thing.' Bathsheba and her mother exchanged glances.

'There, Mother,' she cried. 'I told you he would be like this. I wonder if we could have said what he has. Now, Alec, here is something to take back with you to Scotland. Open it when you come to your father's land and plant them in the spring. If they come up they will help you remember my garden and our spring in the New World.'

Bathsheba's present was a packet of oiled brown paper, and the seeds within it, when planted in the Old World, grew up into flowers and herbs that Alec had either first seen in her garden or in the April forests about York. Some of them flourished and for years to come reminded him of Bathsheba and his sojourn in Canada.

Of their other friends, only Rebecca and Mr. Mackenzie were now lacking. Rebecca had recently left
the Macalisters' service and married Peter, who
worked a struggling farm up in the bush. A week ago
the Buchanans had driven out to say good-bye to her;
on the road Alec had told his father the story of how
she had become 'the girl with an R on her hand'. She
lived too far away to come in and see them off, but
such was not the case with Mr. Mackenzie, who now
came down from his shop and walked out on the
wharf toward them. As he came, Aunt Henrietta and
Cousin Allan stepped off a few feet since they were
not going to be seen with such a radical.

Mr. Mackenzie told them that he would publish
the *Colonial Advocate* again as soon as the new type
he had ordered came from across the border.

'And this lad,' he continued to their father, 'is the
likeliest apprentice I shall ever have had in my shop.
It's a shame you're taking him away from me. This
country needs more lads like him, eh? Well, I can't
persuade you. But perhaps when you're grown up,
Alec, you'll come back to Canada.'

Alec blushed and lost his head with the compliment.
Bathsheba and Aunt Henrietta screamed. 'Watch
out!' cried Charley French, diving into the water at
the same moment, for, unbelievable as it was, Alec
had fallen off the wharf into the water!

The ship's trumpet sounded for the last time, and
with a great deal of laughter and confusion the dripping form of Alec was handed up on board.

As the steamer paddle-wheeled past the lighthouse
and out of the harbour, they met a sailing schooner

from Oswego across the lake just preparing to enter. The lighthouse keeper came out on his balcony and raised a white flag. Joel explained what the white flag meant to his father, while Alec, wrapped up in a blanket, stood at the rail and stared fixedly at the place where he had spent a year that seemed years.

And then the two church spires, the fort, the poplar trees, the line of houses on Palace Street, the street signs, the snow, the muddy streets, the bull's-eye window, the Indians, the soldiers, and the coaches faded away into the autumn haze.

His father tried to hold Alec's hand just in case he might plunge overboard once more, but there was some difficulty.

'Whatever, Alec, have you got so tightly curled up in your hand?'

'It's a piece of type I found once that Mr. Mackenzie's letting me keep. I found it in the water after they threw his type around that time.'

'It's a great capital letter R,' said Joel.

'We'll have to call you the Boy with an R in his Hand,' said his father with a smile.